edited by Timothy Wilson

ASHMOLEAN MUSEUM, OXFORD
2003

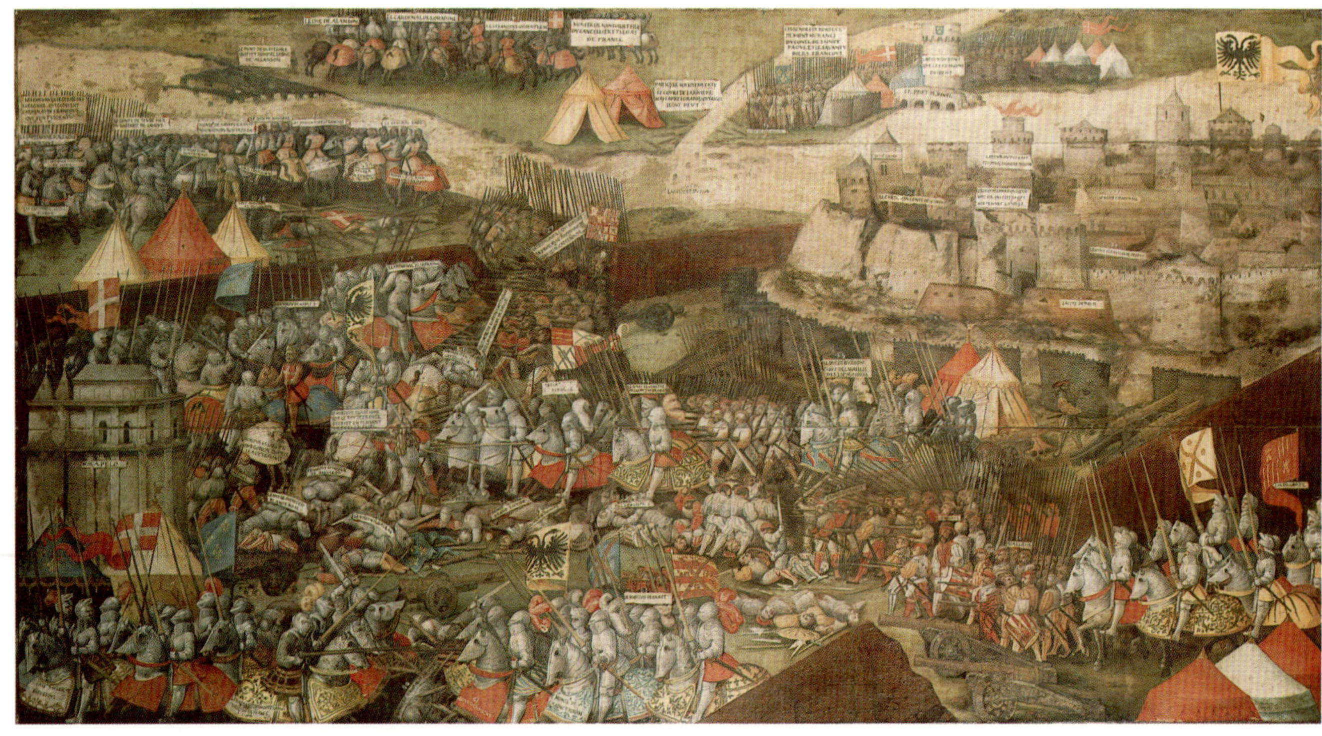

The Battle of Pavia. Perhaps painted in the Burgundian Netherlands, *c.*1525–8.
Presented by Elias Ashmole, 1683 (Ashmolean Museum, F664; WA1908.226.). 117 x 220 cm. Photograph before conservation treatment.

The Battle of Pavia, presented to the University of Oxford in 1683 by Elias Ashmole, is the most spectacular and intriguing of the pictures in the founding collection of the Ashmolean Museum. For many years it had been in visibly poor condition and was one of the pictures in the Museum in most evident need of interventive conservation. The Ashmolean has no picture conservation facilities of its own, but thanks to a grant from the Designation Challenge Fund in 2000 we were able to commission conservation and analytical work in the Hamilton Kerr Institute, University of Cambridge. Additional funding was provided by the Armourers and Brasiers' Gauntlet Trust and the Still Waters Trust.

This booklet is an introduction to the newly resplendent painting. Collaboration between conservators and art-historians has enhanced understanding of the painting, but not all problems have been solved, and research continues.

The Battle of Pavia: the painting as narrative *by Timothy Wilson*

The Battle of Pavia, on 24 February 1525, has been described as marking the end of the Middle Ages. Of the many contemporary artistic representations of this celebrated battle, the painting in the Ashmolean is one of the most detailed, vivid, and ambitiously descriptive.

In the early sixteenth century, Italy was both a battle-ground and a prize in the struggle between the two dominant European powers, France and Spain; the King of Spain was also, in 1525, Holy Roman Emperor. The Battle of Pavia was the culmination of a series of campaigns in Italy, which began when King Charles VIII of France invaded the Spanish kingdom of Naples in 1495, and reached a destructive climax with the sack of Rome by troops of the Empire in 1527.

King Francis I of France shared with Henry VIII of England a ruthless nationalistic ambition, and a love of pomp and chivalric show which found extravagant expression when the two young rulers met at the Field of Cloth of Gold in 1520. The Emperor Charles V had been born in 1500 to an unprecedented inheritance. His grandfather was the Habsburg Emperor Maximilian, his father Philip of Burgundy, and his mother the daughter of Ferdinand and Isabella, king and queen of the newly-united dominions of Spain. Before he was twenty, Charles succeeded to vast possessions in Spain, Austria, the Burgundian Netherlands (mostly in modern Belgium), and Naples; and in 1519 he was elected Holy Roman Emperor.

The French kings had dynastic claims in Italy, both to the kingdom of Naples and to the rich and temptingly accessible duchy of Milan, an Imperial fiefdom of which Pavia formed part. In 1523 Francis had launched an expedition to gain control of Milan, but

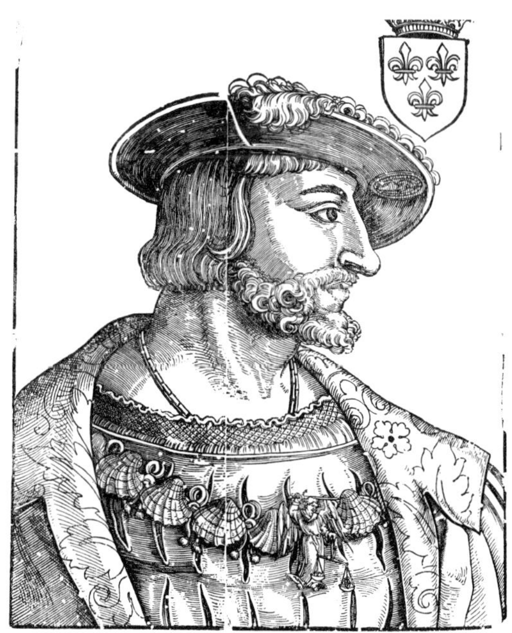

King Francis I of France (1494-1547). A woodcut perhaps made in Paris in the mid-sixteenth century. Ashmolean Museum (Sutherland Collection, BII 625). 33.2 x 27.2 cm

had returned without establishing a power-base there. Meanwhile, he had made a potent enemy at home. Charles, Duke of Bourbon, Constable of France, had been the victim of an attempt to strip him of lands in a lawsuit launched by the Queen Mother; this had driven him into revolt against Francis and into recognizing the claim to the French throne of Henry VIII, whose tortuous diplomacy was veering towards the Imperial side. By 1524 the break was complete and Bourbon became a leader of Imperial armies against Francis. In that year he led a Spanish army to attack Marseilles, but was forced to retreat to Italy.

Francis's expedition into Italy in 1524-5, therefore, was mainly another attempt to make good his claim to Milan, but his aim was also pursuit of the rebellious Duke of Bourbon.

For Francis, war was something of a sport, suffused with vigorous chivalric idealism. However, military technology was changing and this vision of war was obsolescent. In 1495, Charles VIII had taken to Naples a train of horse-drawn field artillery which had impressed the Italians; and firearms of all sorts were becoming a more important factor in warfare. Most important was the arquebus – a portable gun which could be mounted on a forked support to steady its aim. The French armies in the early part of the sixteenth century were strong in artillery, but above all in traditional heavily-armoured cavalry; the charge of such knights and men-at-arms could still under the right circumstances carry all before it, but they were increasingly vulnerable to arquebus fire. The French soldier Montluc, who was to fight at Pavia, noted in 1523 that arquebusiers were rare in French armies and added: "Would to God that this unhappy weapon had never been devised, and that so many brave and valiant men had never died by the hands of those who are often cowards and shirkers, who would never dare to look in the face those whom they lay low with their wretched bullets. They are tools invented by the devil to make it easier for us to kill each other".

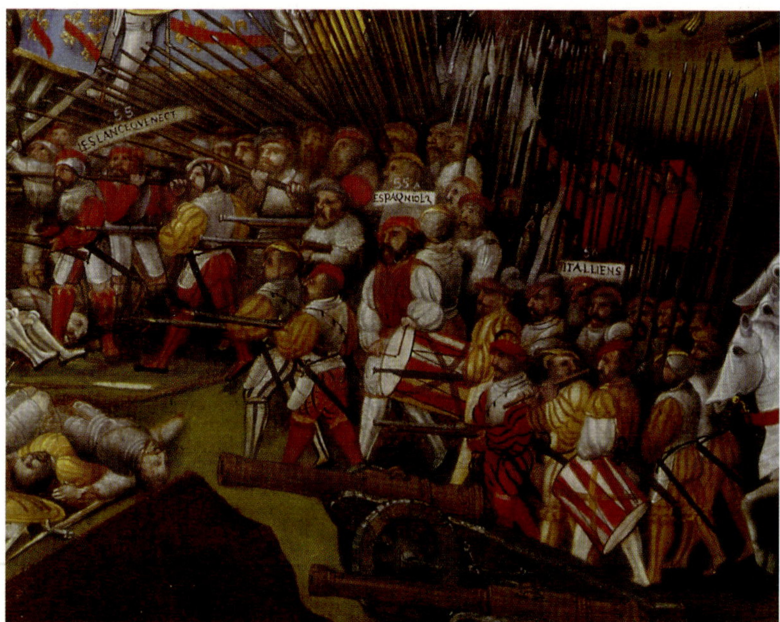

Spanish and Italian arquebusiers on the Imperial side, with pikemen, halbardiers, and artillery.

Characteristic of these Italian wars was the number of mercenaries involved. Swiss infantry pikemen had long been a feared military force, but there were also Italian and Spanish mercenaries, and German infantrymen known as landsknechts. Mercenaries were effective fighters, but notorious for lack of loyalty: if not paid, they would readily abscond or go over to the other side. Both armies at Pavia consisted in great part of mercenaries – Swiss on the French side, and Germans on both sides. Ready supplies of cash were a key strategic issue in such campaigns.

In October 1524, the French army, commanded by Francis himself, crossed the Alps and arrived at Milan. Charles V was safely in Spain, but the Imperial army had capable commanders – Charles de Lannoy (Viceroy of Naples), the Marquis of Pescara, and the Duke of Bourbon. They had retreated from Milan, which was afflicted by plague, leaving a garrison, and soon afterwards arrived before Pavia, which was defended by Imperial troops under the command of the Spanish general Antonio De Leyva.

Francis decided to attack Pavia, but the city was well fortified, and resisted direct assault. An ingenious plan was hatched by the French to divert the river Ticino, which protected one flank of the city, by damming its stream, but the dam was swept away in the winter rains. Francis occupied some comfortable outlying abbeys and the hunting lodge in the park of Mirabello, and settled down to a prolonged blockade. The historian Francesco Guicciardini remarked that the King now largely left military matters to his commander Admiral Bonnivet, "spending most of his time in leisure and empty pleasures, not taking any notice of business or serious planning".

At first the French army outnumbered the enemy. So confident was Francis that he sent off some 15,000 men in an abortive expedition against Naples. This was a result of a secret deal with the new Pope Clement VII, who, in what was to prove a grave misjudgement, leading to the sack of Rome two years later, changed sides from backing the Emperor to supporting the French. Following the defection of a company of Swiss mercenaries, the French army encamped before Pavia was reduced to 20-30,000 men, about the same number as the Imperial forces which Lannoy had gathered near Lodi. Guicciardini noted: "The King paid in his army 1,300 knights, 10,000 Swiss, 4,000 Germans, 5,000 Frenchmen, and 7,000 Italians, although because of the fraud of his captains and the incompetence of his ministers the number of footsoldiers actually active was much smaller".

The siege dragged on from October into February. By that time, inside Pavia, De Leyva (who had already confiscated and melted down the city's church plate) was in crisis from lack of supplies; and the relieving army which Lannoy had moved up towards Pavia was becoming mutinous for the same reason. Guicciardini explained: "The Imperial commanders could not maintain

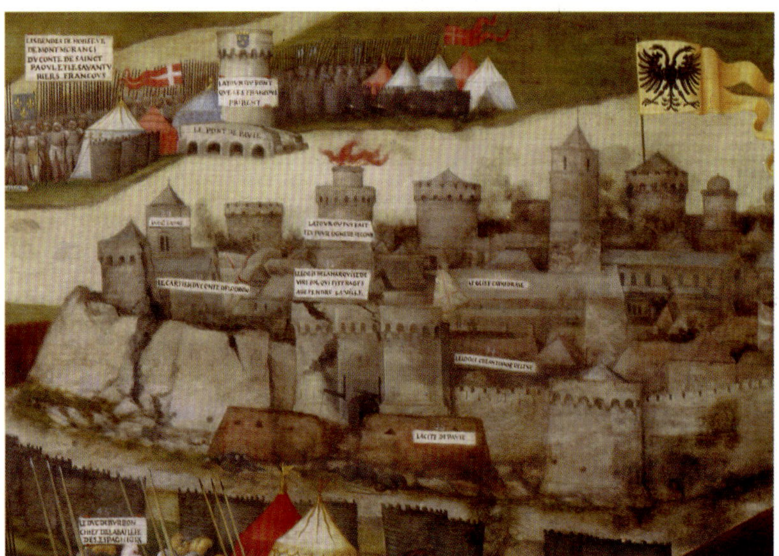

The city of Pavia.

their army any longer... for lack of money. They reckoned that they could not retreat without losing Pavia and also all the other Imperial possessions in the Duchy of Milan. They had good confidence of victory, because of the quality of their troops and the widespread disorder in the French army... They decided to attack...". Lannoy himself, writing to Charles V immediately after the battle, wrote bluntly: "Because of shortage of money we were compelled to come to battle with the King of France".

There are many accounts of the battle, with countless variations and contradictions between them. It was a confused affair, which started with a limited attack by Lannoy's army to link up with a sortie from the city. In the dark small hours of a February morning, it grew into a full-scale battle, which was over by 9 o'clock, before the morning mist had cleared. Not even the participants knew much about what was going on. Discovering what actually happened is further complicated by the fact that most contemporary accounts were slanted to make a point, or to glorify or blame a particular individual.

Operations opened on the night of 23/ 24 February, when Imperial sappers made breaches in the wall round the park. The alarm was raised slowly and a detachment of Imperial arquebusiers under the Marquis of Vasto was able to enter the park. Other troops followed, and the Imperialists rapidly captured Mirabello and came to outnumber the French in key scenes of action. By this time the main units of French cavalry, including the King himself, were alerted: they arrived on the scene, charged and routed the Imperial cavalry, and were left in possession of a sodden piece of ground flanked by woods and ditches. At this point Francis seems to have thought he had won: he is reported to have said to one of his knights: "Now I can really call myself the Duke of Milan". In reality, the French cavalry were isolated from supporting infantry, handicapped by poor visibility, and trapped on ground which restricted their mobility. Exposed to lethal flanking fire from arquebusiers screened by trees, and attacked by infantry, "the nobility and gentry of France fell like ripe pears".

A letter written the day after the battle by the papal nuncio Bernardino Castellaro tells how "the King's horse was killed beneath him, and so he was taken prisoner, lightly wounded in one hand and less seriously in the face. There is great dispute about who took him prisoner, and there are many who claim to have done so. One says that he killed the King's horse under him; another that he took his sword and gauntlet from him; another that he pulled him from the horse by his helmet; and others claim this and that... Suffice it to say that the Viceroy of Naples ran to the noise and took charge of him with respect, keeping away those around him". One account gives the following words to the King as he yielded to Lannoy: "Don Charles, here is the sword of a King who has earned praise, because before giving it up he has spilt the blood of many of your men; so he has been taken prisoner, not through cowardice, but through ill fortune".

Among those killed near the King were several of the greatest nobles of France, including Jacques de La Palisse and Louis de la Trémouille (Marshals of France), the "Bastard of Savoy" (Grand Master of France), and Admiral Bonnivet, Francis's most trusted military adviser. It was the greatest disaster for French chivalry since Agincourt. Among others killed was Richard de la Pole, self-styled Duke of Suffolk, pretender to the throne of England.

Meanwhile the Swiss mercenaries of the French army were overwhelmed by landsknechts and fled. The French rearguard under the Duke of Alençon never got into action at all and retreated beyond the Ticino. By breaking the bridge behind them they avoided pursuit but cut off the escape of many of their own side, who were drowned trying to cross the river. In all, the French army may have lost as many as ten thousand men.

After the battle, Francis was shown exaggerated chivalrous respect by Lannoy and Bourbon. He wrote to his mother with famous words: "Madam. To inform you of how the rest of my ill fortune is proceeding, all is lost to me but honour and life..."
He was released the following year, having signed the Treaty of Madrid, committing himself to cede Burgundy to Charles. As soon as he was safely back in France, he obtained permission from the Pope to repudiate the pledge; but French ambitions in Italy never recovered from Pavia. Milan and Naples remained under Imperial control. The Duke of Bourbon became Duke of Milan, but was killed two years later at the siege of Rome (Benvenuto Cellini claimed to have shot him). In 1529 the Peace of Cambrai finally brought the campaigns in Italy to an end.

The dramatic outcome of the battle and the capture of the King resonated through Europe. Written descriptions are matched by numerous visual representations - paintings, prints, and tapestries. A series of seven magnificent tapestries, designed by Bernard van Orley, was woven in Brussels and presented to Charles in 1531; they are now at Capodimonte. Several of the surviving paintings have been for centuries in England (possibly reflecting English glee at the discomfiture of Henry VIII's great rival, the King of France), including examples in the Royal Collection and at Wilton House. One formerly at Cowdray was destroyed by fire in 1793.

In the Ashmolean picture, events that actually took place at different times are presented simultaneously. No character appears more than once, but the artist has contrived to get in as many details as possible. Painted on to the surface, as if on labels fixed with red sealing-wax, are descriptive captions in erratic French. In the nineteenth century, numbers were painted on, for reference to an explanatory key. A new key, using these numbers, is on pp. 9–11.

The topography bears little relationship to the lie of the land at Pavia, and it seems unlikely that the artist had seen the city. The painting looks like a diagrammatic illustration to a text, cramming in information at some cost to lucidity. However, no written account of the battle has yet been found which corresponds closely enough with the details in the painting to have provided its programme.

It seems likely that the picture was painted for a recipient with a special interest in the battle, probably someone linked to the Imperial side, which is shown in a more dignified light.

Another painting of the battle (p. 15), now in the Royal Armouries at Leeds, is similar in style and in many details to the Ashmolean picture. Woodhouse and Woudhuysen-Keller (below) conclude, on the basis of technical analysis of the underdrawing, that the Ashmolean picture was painted in the same workshop, but after the Armouries one. The differences probably reflect the interests of the patrons or intended recipients. Although the same drawings seem to have been used, the characters and incidents differ; in general the Ashmolean picture is more consistently anti-French. In the Armouries picture the captions are in Italian, but in the Ashmolean version in French, presumably reflecting the first language of the intended recipient. The alarming spelling of the French, on the other hand, might suggest that French was not the native language of whoever wrote the inscriptions; the confusion of the letters *V* and *Y* is one of several mistakes suggesting the painter was copying words in a language not his own.

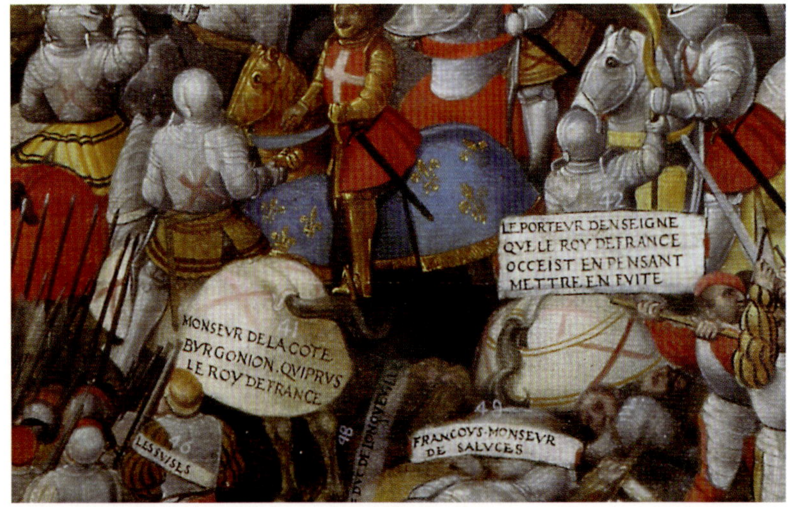

The capture of Francis I by Monsieur de la Motte. The King wears gilded armour and has the white cross of France (a national emblem, like Saint George's cross for England) on his chest. To the right of the King is "the standard-bearer the King killed". DE LA COTE, as here shown, is a mis-restoration and has subsequently been corrected to DE LA MOTE.

Key to *The Battle of Pavia*

Participants on the French side are marked **[F]**, those on the Emperor's **[E]**.

1. LE PONT DE BVFFELORE QVI FIST ROMPRE LE DVC DE ALLANSON (Buffelore bridge, which the Duke of Alençon caused to be broken down).
2. LE DVC DE ALANSON (Charles, Duke of Alençon, 1489–1525, husband of Francis' sister Marguerite. Escaped). **[F]**
3. LE CARDINAL DE LORAINNE (Jean de Guise, 1498–1550; Cardinal from 1518). **[F]**
4. LES FRANCOYS QVI SENFVIENT (the French in flight).
5. MONSER DE NANTOLLIET FILZ DV CANCELLIER ET LEGAT DE FRANCE (Antoine Duprat, Lord of Nantouillet and Précy, *c.*1495–1553, son of Antoine Duprat, Chancellor of France). **[F]**
6. LES BENDES DE MONSEVR DE MONTMORANCI DV CONTE DE SAINCT PAOVL ET LES AVANTVRIERS FRANCOVS (the companies of François de Montmorency, d.1551, brother of no. **20**; and those of François Count of Saint-Pol, no. **22**; and the French adventurers). **[F]**
7. LA TOVR DV PONT QVE LES FRANCOVS PRIRENT (the bridge tower captured by the French).
8. PAR ICY LE VOVLOIT DIVERTY LE COVRS DE LA RIVIERE MAYS APRES GRANIZ COVTAIGES IL NE PEVT (here [the French] wanted to divert the river but failed despite great efforts).
9. LISLE DE GRAVALLON (the island of Gravellone).
10. LE PONT DE PAVIE (Pavia bridge).
11. LES CHEVAVLX LEGIERS DES ESPAGNIOL QVI COPIRENT CHEMIN AVIX FRANCOVS QVI SEN FVIOENT (the Spanish light cavalry who intercepted the fleeing French).
12. LE CONTE DE TENDE FILZ DV BASTARD DE SAVOYE (Claude of Savoy, 1507–66, Count of Tende and Villars, son of no. **59**. Captured). **[F]**
13. MONSE[R] DE GRVFFY GRAND MIGNION DY ROY DE FRAN (the Lord of Gruffy [in Switzerland], d. 1528, Favourite of the King of France. Captured). **[F]**
14. LE ROY DE NAVARRE (Henri d'Albret, 1503–55, succeeded to throne of Navarre 1516. Captured). **[F]**
15. LES PRISONNIERS FRANCOYS (French prisoners).
16. LE PRINCE DE TALMONT (François de la Trémouille, Prince of Talmont, *c.*1503–41, grandson of no. **39**. Captured). **[F]**
17. LE GENERAL BABO (Philibert Babou, Lord of La Bourdaisière and Thuisseau, 1485–1557, Treasurer of France. Captured). **[F]**
18. LE CAPITAINNE SCALENGVE PIEMONTOVS (Giacomo di Scalenghe, Governor of Asti). **[E]**
19. LE CAPITAINNE PONTVOYRE DE SAYOYE (François de Montchenu, Lord of Ternier and Pontverre, d.1529). **[E]**
20. LE MARESCAL MONTMORENCI (Anne de Montmorency, 1493–1567, Marshal of France. Captured). **[F]**
21. LOROL CAPITAINNE (possibly François de Loriol, Lord of Saint André du Bouchoux and of La Tour Neuville). **[F]**
22. LE CONTE DE SAINCT PAOVL (François de Bourbon-Vendôme, Count of Saint-Pol, 1491–1545. Wounded, captured, later escaped). **[F]**
23. NONSER DE FLORANGES (Robert III de la Marck, 1491–1537, Lord of Fleuranges, known as *Le Jeune Aventureux*. Captured). **[F]**

24. MONSEVR DE RIAN SAVOSIEN (possibly François de la Forest, Lord of Rians). **[F]**
25. LE CAPITAINNE SVCRE FLAMEN (Jacques de Succre, Lord of Bellaing, *c.*1485–1535). **[E]**
26. LOYS MONSEVR DE NEVERS (Louis de Clèves, or de Nevers, Count of Auxerre, *c.*1495–1545. Captured). **[F]**
27. LES ESPAGNIOLZ QVI SORTIRET DE PAVIE AVEC ANTOINNE DE LEVA LEVR CAPITAINNE (the Spaniards under Antonio De Leyva, *c.*1480–1536, commander of the Pavia garrison, making a sortie from Pavia). **[E]**
28. LA RIVIERE DV TISIN (River Ticino).
29. SAINCT LADRE (the church of San Lazzaro).
30. LE CARTIER DV CONTE DE LODRON (the headquarters of the Count of Lodron; see no. **38**).
31. LA TOVR OV FVT FAIT FEV POUR SIGNE DE SECOVR (the tower from which a beacon signal for help was made).
32. LE LOGIS DE LA MARQUISE DE VIRESOL QVI FIST RAGES A DEFENDRE LA VILLE (the lodgings of Ippolita Malaspina, Marchioness of Scaldasole, who made passionate efforts to defend the city). **[E]**
33. LEGLISE CATHEDRALE (Pavia cathedral).
34. LES LOGISC DE ANTOINNE DE LEVE (the lodgings of Antonio De Leyva, no. **27**).
35. LA CITE DE PAVIE (the city of Pavia).
36. LE VISROY DE NAPLES (Charles de Lannoy, 1482–1527, Commander of the Imperial Armies in Italy, Viceroy of Naples). **[E]**
37. LERRI MONSE[R] DE LOARRAINE (probably François de Lorraine, Lord of Lambesc, 1506–25. Killed). **[F]**
38. LE CONTE DE LORON CAPITAINNE DES LANSQVENEST DE PAVIE (Ludwig, Count of Lodron,1484–1537, a landsknecht commander). **[E]**
39. MODISE[R] DE LATRIMOQLIE (Louis II de la Tremouille, 1460–1525, Viscount of Thouars. Killed). **[F]**
40. MIRAPELO (the Lodge of Mirabello).
41. MONSEVR DE LA MOTE BVRGONION. QVI PRVS LE ROY DE FRANCE (Monsieur de la Motte-de-Noyers, a follower of Bourbon, who claimed to have captured the King). **[E]**
42. LE PORTEVR DENSEIGNE QVE LE ROY DE FRANCE OCCEIST EN PENSANT METTRE EN FVITE (the standard bearer whom the King of France killed; possibly the standard bearer of Niklas, Count of Salm-Reifferscheidt, leader of a company sent by the Archduke of Austria). **[E]**
43. LE MARQUIS DE PISGAIRE (Ferdinando Francesco d'Avalos, Marquis of Pescara, 1490–1525, Commander of the Imperial army in Lombardy). **[E]**
44. LE CONTE DE GENEFVE FRERE DV DVC DE SAVOYE (Philippe, Count of Geneva, 1490–1533, brother of Charles, Duke of Savoy). **[E]**
45. LE DVC DE BVRBON CHIEF DE LA BATLLIE DES ESPAGNIOLZ (Charles, Duke of Bourbon, 1490–1527, Imperial commander). **[E]**
46. LES SVISES (Swiss). **[F]**
47. LE DVC DE SVSFOC DIT BLANCE ROSE (Richard de la Pole, self-styled Duke of Suffolk, pretender to the English throne, known as "White Rose". Killed). **[F]**
48. LE DVC DE LONQVEVILLE (Louis, Duke of Longueville, 1510–36). **[F]**
49. FRANCOYS MONSEVR DE SALVCES (François de Saluces, 1490–1537. Captured). **[F]**
50. LE VISCONTE GALEAS (Galeazzo Visconti, Duke of Bari, d.1537, Chamberlain of Francis I. Captured). **[F]**
51. MONSE[R] DE LESCV (Thomas de Foix, Lord of Lescun, *c.*1485–1525, Marshal of France. Died of wounds at Milan after the battle). **[F]**

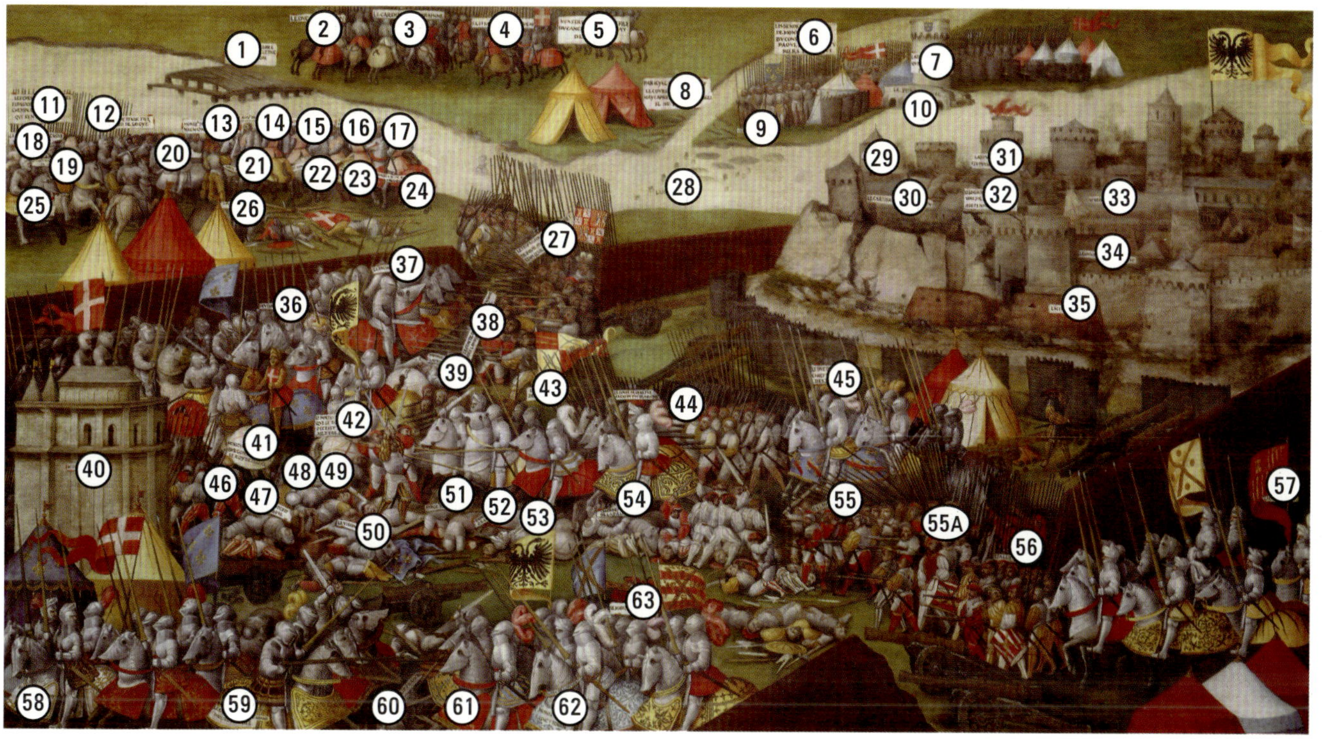

52. SAINEE SEVERIN GRAND ESCVIER (Galeazzo di San Severino, Count of Voghera, *c.*1470–1525, Grand Esquire of France. Killed). **[F]**
53. LE CONTE DE TONNOIRE (Claude de Husson, Count of Tonnerre. Killed). **[F]**
54. MONSE^{R} DE LA PALISSE (Jacques II de Chabannes, 1465–1525, Lord of La Palisse. Killed). **[F]**
55. LES LANCEQVENECT (landsknechts). **[E]**
55A. ESPAQNIOLZ (Spaniards). **[E]**
56. ITALLIENS (Italians). **[E]**
57. LARRIEGARDE (the Imperial rearguard). **[E]**
58. MONSE^{R} DAVEBIGNY ESCOSSOYS (the Scotsman Robert Stuart, Lord of Aubigny, *c.*1470-1544. Captured). **[F]**
59. LE BASTARD DE SAVOYE GRAND MAISTRE DE FRANCE (René, Count of Tende and Villars, 1473–1525, Grand Master of France, natural son of Philip II, Duke of Savoy. Died of wounds soon after the battle). **[F]**
60. BONIVET ADMIRAL DE FRANCE (Guillaume Gouffier, Lord of Bonnivet, *c.*1488–1525, Admiral of France. Killed). **[F]**
61. BOVRGONNIONS (Burgundians). **[E]**
62. MONSE^{R} DE SAINCT SORLIN (probably Claude de la Baume, Baron of Saint-Sorlin, *c.*1480–*c.*1541). **[E]**
63. LE MARQVIS DE GVAST (Alfonso d'Avalos, Marquis of Vasto, 1502–46). **[E]**

Adapted from G. Taylor's account in *Tradescant's Rarities* (1983), with additional research by Roger Middleton.

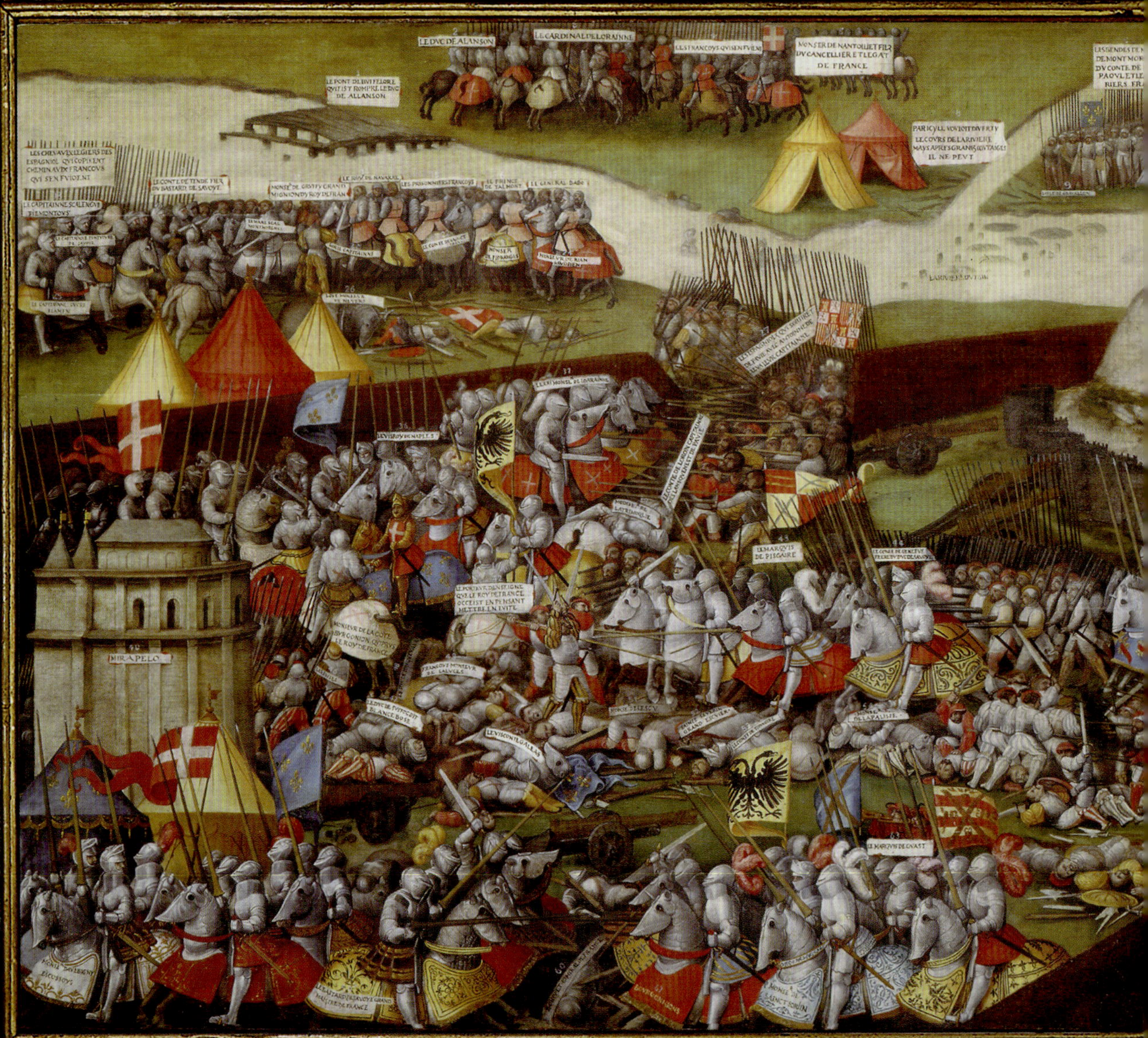
62. LE VRAY PORTRAIT DV SIEGE DE PAVIE MIST SVR LA FIN D OCTOBRE
LE DVC DE ALANSON
LE CARDINAL DE LORAINNE
MIRAPELO
COMMEN LES GENS DE LEMPEREVR DEFFIRENT LES FRANCOYS EN PREGNANT LE ROY

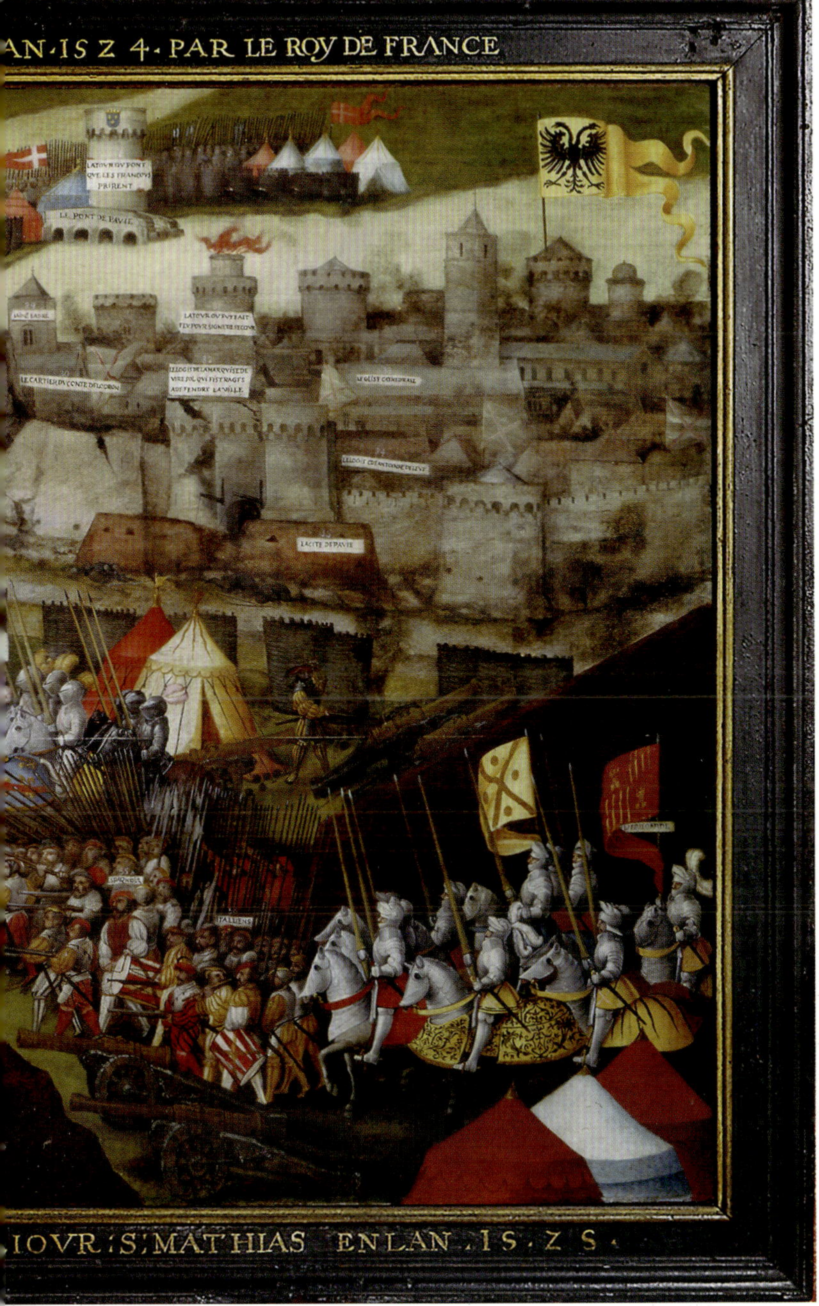

The Battle of Pavia

On the right is the many-towered city of Pavia, with a banner of the double-headed Imperial eagle and a signal fire on top of one of the towers. Past it flows the river Ticino, with three broken-down bridges. By the inlet top centre is a label recording that it was here that the French attempted to divert the river. On the right are the breaches in the park wall, through which come Imperial soldiers led by the Duke of Bourbon. To the left is the lodge of Mirabello. Nearby is the capture of King Francis, his horse bedecked with the fleurs-de-lis of France. Above left is a group of captured French prisoners. Bottom centre is a cavalry engagement with the death of Admiral Bonnivet. Bottom right is the unhurried approach of the Imperial rearguard, with Spanish banners. At the top the Duke of Alençon and the Cardinal of Lorraine lead their men away from the battle in a dishonourable-looking way.

The frame is early, probably original to the painting, but has been extended with a later moulding. Its inscription in French, probably of sixteenth-century origin, translates: "The true picture of the Siege of Pavia, begun at the end of October 1524 by the King of France. How the Emperor's people defeated the French and captured the King on St Matthias' day in the year 1525".

Photograph after conservation

The key to the commission of the Ashmolean picture may be the conspicuous presence, at the very centre, of "the Count of Geneva, brother of the Duke of Savoy", who rides splendidly caparisoned just behind the triumphant Marquis of Pescara and tramples under his horse's feet a renowned French casualty, Jacques de La Palisse. This Count of Geneva was Philip, the brother of Charles III, Duke of Savoy. He is not prominent in contemporary accounts of the battle, but he mattered in the Emperor's family. In his dispatch to Charles V immediately after the battle, Lannoy specially noted that "the Count of Geneva had his horse killed beneath him by artillery, but is unharmed". From 1501 until his early death in 1504, his half brother Philibert, the previous Duke of Savoy, had been married to Margaret of Austria, Charles V's aunt. In 1525 Margaret was Regent of the Netherlands on behalf of Charles V; she was violently anti-French, and among those who rejoiced at the victory. This prompts the thought that our painting could have been painted for Margaret or someone in her circle, or, since other figures associated with Savoy are also prominent, for someone with Savoyard connections. In a note to an inventory of Margaret's possessions at Malines made in 1531, a painting of the battle is listed. However, the idea that this could have been the Ashmolean painting is refuted by the fact that the inventory describes it as on canvas, not wood. The only known surviving picture on canvas is one (perhaps not as early as 1531) formerly at Cobham Hall, and subsequently in the hands of the Italian dealers Margua; its present location is unknown.

The picture in the Royal Armouries has as its pivotal figure the "Conte de Giarva". This individual remains unidentified: it has been suggested he is meant to be the same Count of Geneva as in the Ashmolean picture, but he is shown with a French royal banner, standing over the French artillery, so it is logical to suppose him on the French side; were it not for the inscription, one might guess him to be Jacques Galliot, Grand Master of French artillery. It may be that his identity is the key to the commissioning of the Leeds painting.

The prominence afforded in the Ashmolean painting to the Count of Geneva provides a possible clue to the date of the

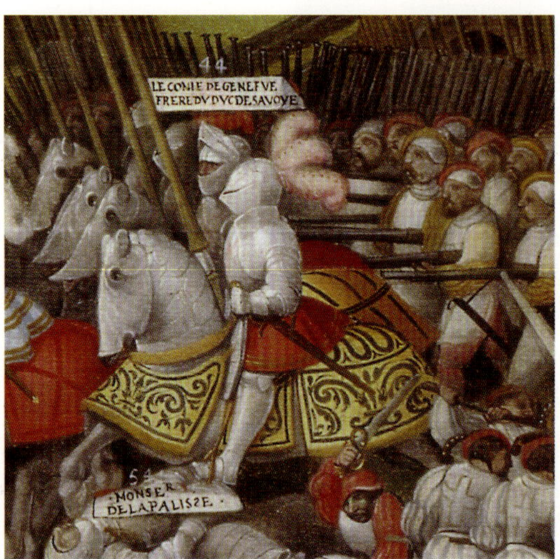

Philip, Count of Geneva.

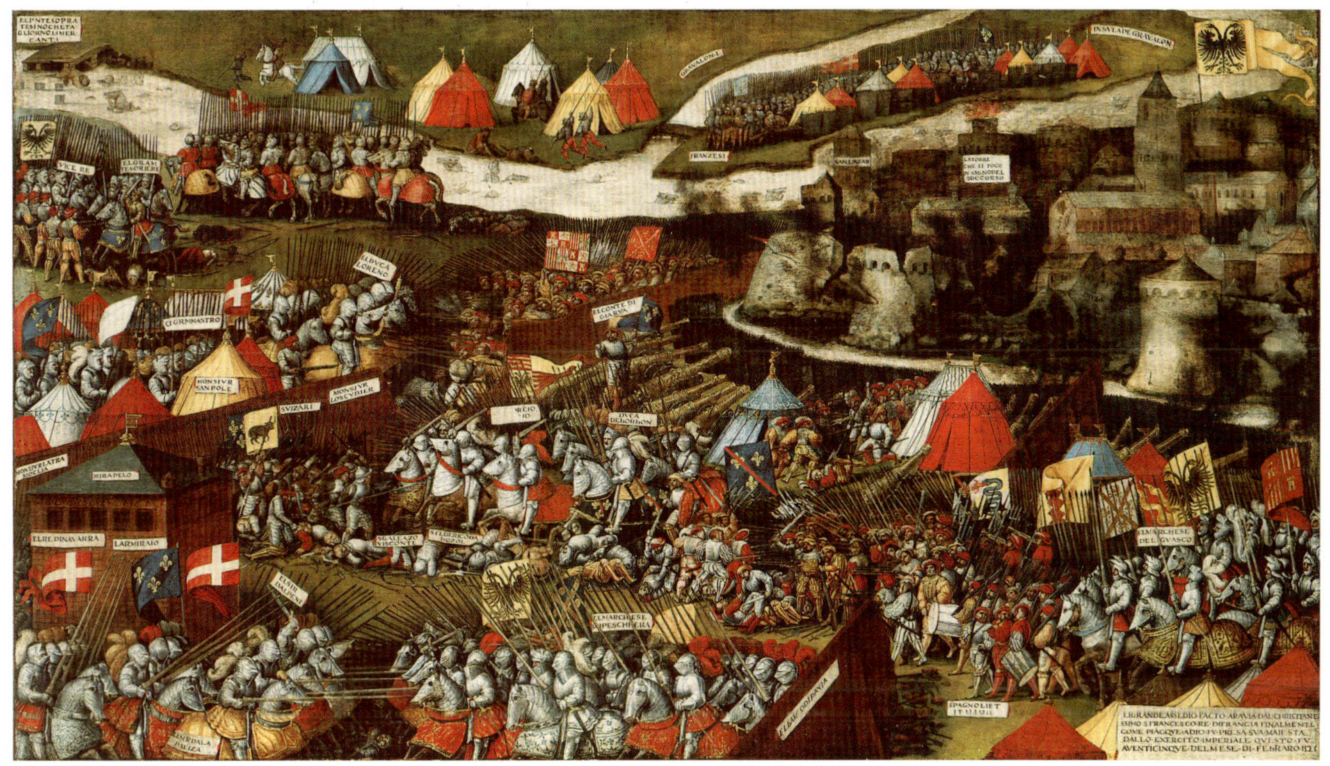

two paintings. At Pavia, Philip fought on the Imperial side. Three years later, he changed sides and was made Duke of Nemours by Francis. In view of the Imperial sympathies of the painting, it may be considered unlikely that a turncoat would have been given this prominence; this suggests the painting is likely to have been made before 1528. A dating of 1525–8 is (just) consistent with the dendrochronological evidence (see p. 21).

The attribution of the two pictures remains a problem. The composition of our picture bears no relation to the norms of composing battle paintings in Italy, and the fact that the planks on which it is painted are of Baltic oak indicates an origin north of the Alps. The closest analogy in style which has been found – perhaps by the same artist – is a painting at Hampton Court of *The Meeting of Henry VIII and the Emperor Maximilian* (p. 16), which is catalogued as "probably by a Flemish painter".

The Hampton Court painting was among many paintings of battles and contemporary events which belonged to Henry VIII. Notwithstanding the reasons given above suggesting a Burgundian or Savoyard

The Battle of Pavia.
Royal Armouries, Leeds.
118.1 x 207.6 cm.

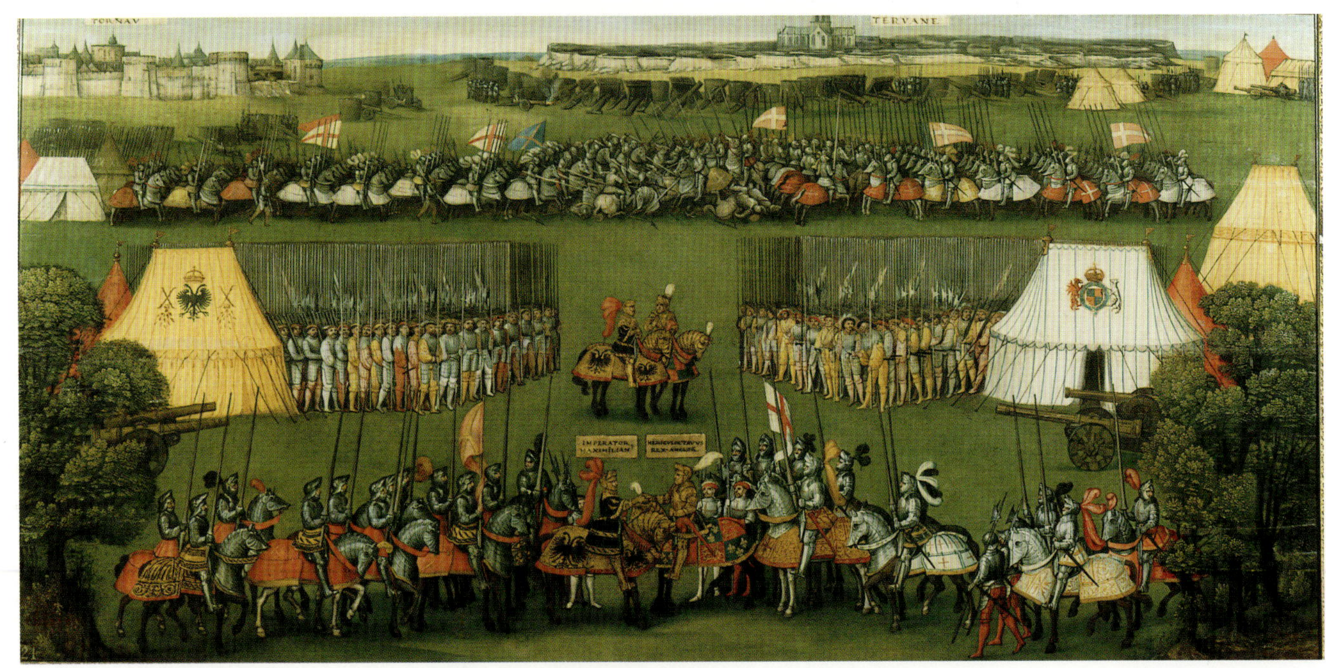

link, it is possible that *The Battle of Pavia* has been in England since soon after it was painted. The inventory of Henry's possessions made after his death in 1547 included, among the "Tables with pictures" at Whitehall, a "Table with the Siege of Pavie with a curteyne of yellowe and white" (as well as, among his "Mappes", a "Discription of the Siege of pavie when ye frenche kynge was taken beinge of Lynnen clothe stayned"). However, no evidence has been found that this "Table" was the Ashmolean picture, rather than another version.

In the present state of knowledge, somewhere in the Southern Netherlands seems the most likely location for the workshop of the Ashmolean painting, though the realms of the Duke of Savoy are an intriguing alternative hypothesis. The artist may have been not so much a specialist in easel painting as a herald-painter, or a painter of maps - this would be consistent with the care taken to paint accurately the banners, heraldry, arms, and armour. Such work is seldom signed and notoriously difficult to attribute. *The Battle of Pavia* has many secrets to yield up to future research.

The Meeting of Henry VIII and the Emperor Maximilian. Panel, attributed to a 16th-century Flemish artist, perhaps by the painter of *The Battle of Pavia*. 99.1 x 205.7 cm. [The Royal Collection. © 2003, Her Majesty Queen Elizabeth II]

The Battle of Pavia and the Tradescant pictures *by Arthur MacGregor*

The collection history of the picture proves at first promising but ends in tantalizing uncertainty. What is clear is that the undisputed record of *The Battle of Pavia*'s presence in Oxford can be extended back to the earliest years following the Museum's foundation in 1683.

Amongst the regulations drawn up by Elias Ashmole for his new institution was a requirement that a catalogue should be drawn up of the entire collection and that "the said catalogue be divided into parts according to the number of Visitors [the Museum's governing body] ... each Visitor comparing his part & seeing that all particulars are safe and well conditioned, & answering to the catalogue". Within one of these volumes we find an accurate transcription of the painted legend that survives on the frame today, *Le vray portrait du Siege de Pavie*, etc.

The incontrovertible record of the picture in this early source carries with it the strong implication that, like most of the other material in the Museum's foundation collection, *The Battle of Pavia* came from the Tradescant collection, items from which formed the bulk of Ashmole's benefaction. Early visitors to the Tradescant museum at Lambeth had been shown, amongst a huge range of other rarities, "diverse curiosities in carving and painting", but there is a lack of helpful detail in all the surviving accounts. The first comprehensive overview of the collection comes in the form of a printed catalogue of 1656, where we find an entry for "Severall draughts and pieces of painting

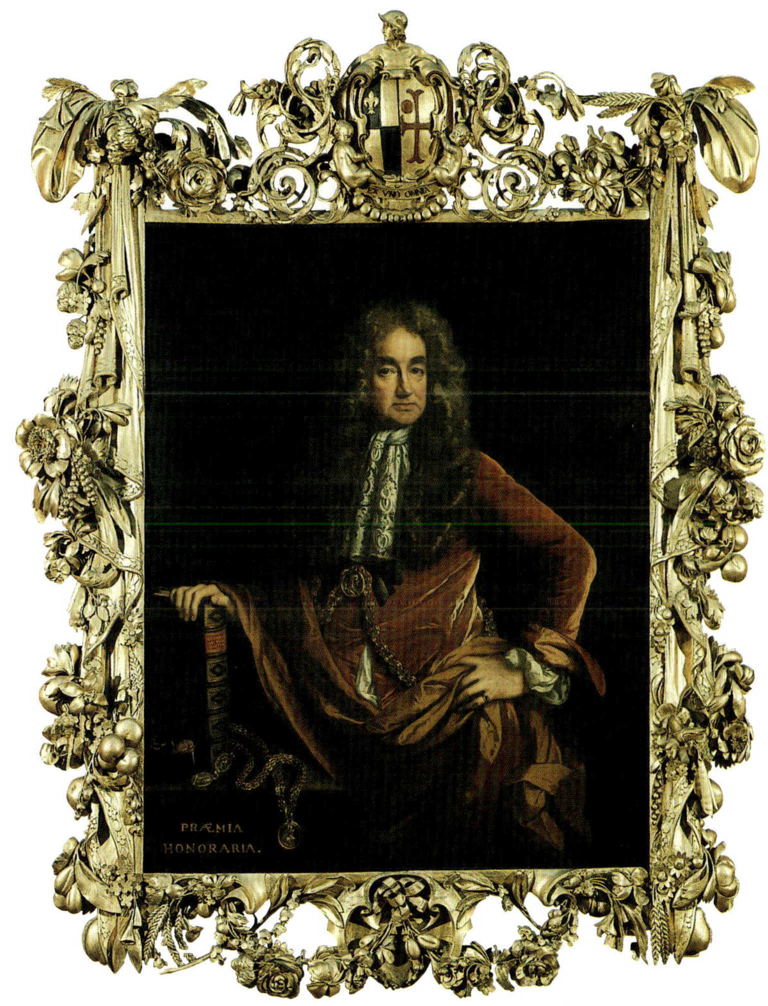

Portrait of Elias Ashmole, by John Riley, *c.*1682. The carved frame is by Grinling Gibbons. Overall 188 x 148 cm. Ashmolean Museum, F730.

of sundry excellent Masters" – scarcely conclusive evidence for the presence of our picture. None of the Tradescant family portraits now in the Ashmolean is listed in the catalogue, however, so the pictures hanging in the private areas of the house evidently escaped the attentions of the cataloguers. Could *The Battle of Pavia* have been one of these? Possibly, and we must also remember that Tradescant the Younger lived (and no doubt collected) for a further six years after publication of the catalogue, so that the significance of its absence from this text is at least ambivalent.

Other items among the Ashmolean's early exhibits came from Ashmole's own collection. Most of these arrived by bequest at the time of his death in 1692: consisting exclusively of portraits, depicting Ashmole himself, members of the royal family, and various learned subjects (notably scholars with strong astrological leanings such as John Dee and William Lilly), they reflect accurately the world that Ashmole saw himself as occupying. We can well imagine, too, that *The Battle of Pavia*, with its dense programme of heraldry and its references to many of the noble households of Europe, would have had a strong appeal to Ashmole, one time Windsor Herald and author of an impressive *History of the Order of the Garter.* Ashmole's personal contributions to the museum are comparatively well-documented, however, and nowhere do we find any mention of the picture. This seems a more significant deficit, and it is hard to believe that such a gift would have escaped all record had it indeed come directly from the founder to his Museum.

Finally, it may be mentioned that benefactions from other donors began to arrive as soon as the Ashmolean was established, opening up a third possible route by which *The Battle of Pavia* could have entered the collections. In the early years of its administration, however, the keepers of the Museum were assiduous in recording all such gifts in an elaborate *Book of Benefactors*; the names of such benefactors were also included with the appropriate entries in the Visitors' catalogues referred to above. The absence of any reference to the picture in the *Book of Benefactors* and the lack of a donor's name in the catalogue entry already quoted would seem to exclude the possibility of its having been given by an independent donor.

On balance, therefore, the most likely route by which the painting reached the Ashmolean remains the Tradescant collection, although how it came into the possession of these royal gardeners, father and son, remains entirely unresolved.

Conservation and observations about the painting technique of *The Battle of Pavia* and its counterpart in the Royal Armouries

by Hayley Woodhouse and Renate Woudhuysen-Keller

Consolidation and cleaning

When *The Battle of Pavia* arrived at the Hamilton Kerr Institute it was covered in layers of grey dirt and yellow varnish. The paint-layer was lifting off its panel like countless scales with raised edges and threatening to fall off at any moment. Large old fillings and retouchings suggested that there had been paint losses before and that the paint-layer's tendency to flake had been an old and ongoing problem. A solution of sturgeon glue in water was allowed to run through the cracks underneath the paint-layer, which was then smoothed down and dried with a warm spatula. After removal of dirt and varnish layers, previous retouchings and fillings were removed. The paint-layer then appeared in its original luminosity and splendour. Luckily the damage was limited to well-defined paint losses and there was little abrasion of the painted surface.

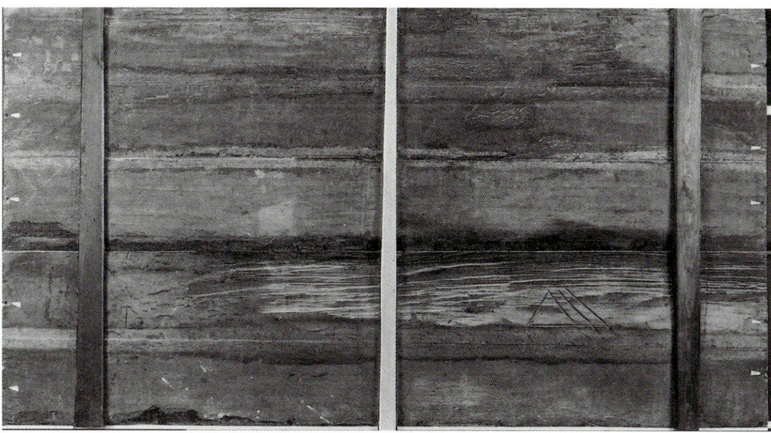

Backof the panel after conservation treatment.

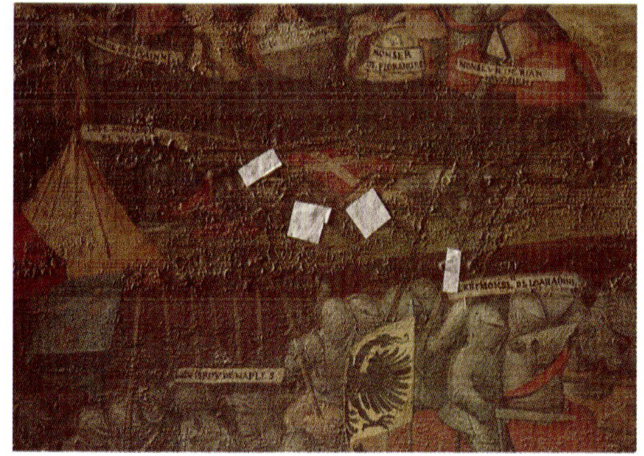

Detail of *The Battle of Pavia* before treatment, raking light photograph of detail upper left, showing raised paintlayer.

Structural work

After consolidation and cleaning the structural problems of the panel were dealt with. The panel consists of five oak boards joined horizontally. Our main concern was the third join from the top. It became clear that at some point this had come apart and had been rejoined. There were a visually disturbing step and gap between these boards, filled with a previous restorer's putty. The first action in dealing with this was to take the boards apart. Next, the old glue and putty had to be removed. We experimented whether it would be possible to eliminate the step using a bridge system developed by Ray Marchant. The painting was placed flat on raised supports and the bridge positioned over it. Flexible wooden props on small cushions were then wedged between bridge and panel and between panel and table in order to manipulate the boards into the best position. The edges of the boards were then glued and the panel rejoined.

Rejoining the panel – application of gentle pressure with small props on either side of the join to achieve a proper alignment.

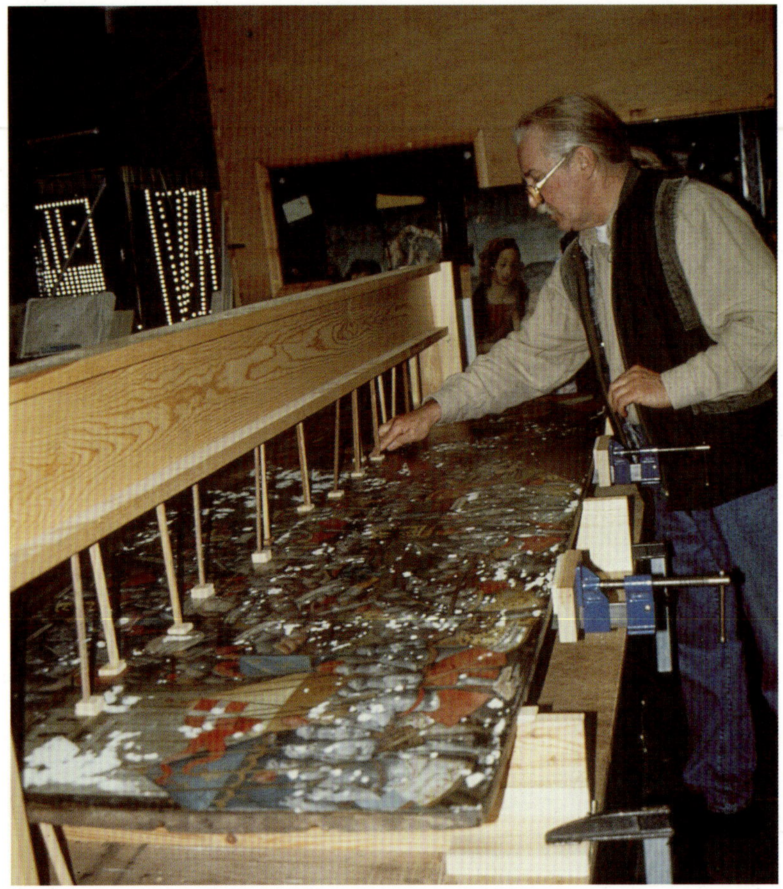

Filling and retouching

The last stage of conservation treatment is filling and retouching. This is the part of conservation that can most correctly be called restoration, when an attempt is made to make good the losses with retouchings to complete the original image again. Although in certain situations it may be appropriate to leave losses to some extent visible, it was decided in this case to attempt a matching finish. However, fashions may change and future generations may no longer find this approach acceptable. This is the main reason for using reversible materials: i.e. those that can be easily removed at a later date without damage to the original. First the losses are filled to make them level with the original paint surface. Then the fillings are textured to make them blend in perfectly. A view of the painting after filling, but before retouching, illustrates the extent of the losses (p.21). Retouching – or in-painting – is then done on top of the textured fillings, separated by an intermediate varnish. Until the early part of the twentieth century the most commonly used retouching medium was oil. However, not only is this not easily reversible, but it also discolours, as was the case with the previous oil-paint retouchings. The medium used most at the Hamilton Kerr

Institute is egg-tempera. Whole egg is used with a little water added. Egg-tempera is both reversible and stable. It can be applied in very thin layers, then burnished with an agate, thus imitating the effect of aged layers of oil-paint. Contrary to what is sometimes thought, it is not enough to simply mix the colour to match the surrounding original and then paint it on to the filling. The tonal effect of the original paint is very difficult to match without reconstructing the entire original layer structure: the ground colour, the underlayers, the resinous glazes on top. The resin used for glazes on top of the egg-tempera is synthetic, the same as that used for the varnish layers, and it is reversible and stable. The restoration completed, the painting was then varnished.

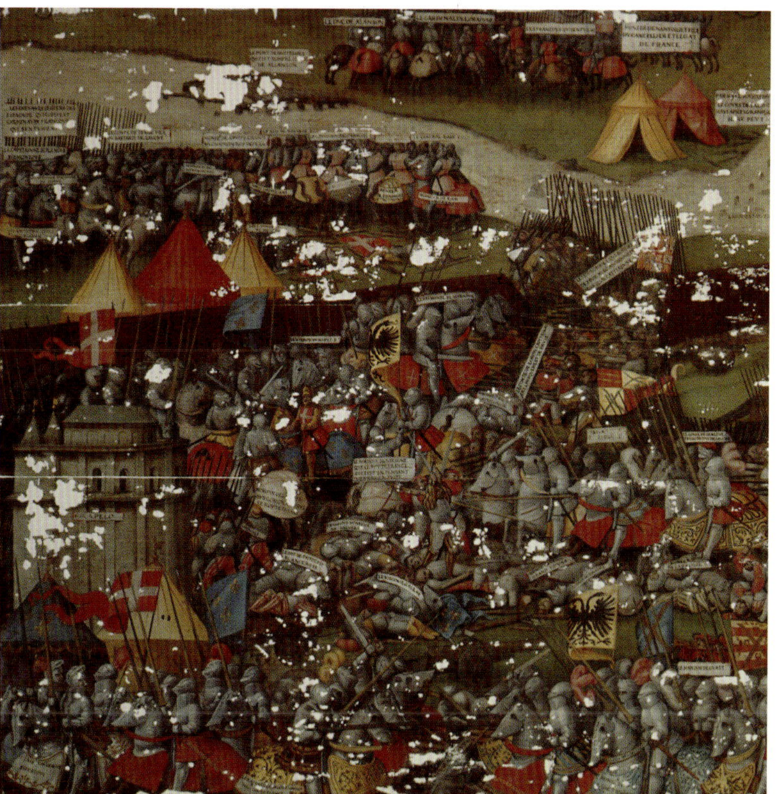

The Battle of Pavia, left-hand half, after cleaning and filling, before retouching.

Painting technique

Restoration provides an opportunity to study the painting technique and materials used. The five boards of the panel were glued together without using dowels. Three vertical battens were slotted into dove-tail grooves at the back to provide extra support. By the method of dendrochronology – comparing growth patterns of annual tree-rings – the date for the felling of the trees used for making the boards can be put some time between 1522 and 1545. Considering the suggestion above (p. 15) that the painting might have been commissioned soon after 1525, this leaves a very short time for seasoning the timber. Priming and paint-layers are as thin and smooth as is characteristic for a painting of the first half of the 16th century. In the river and in the town the texture and warm tone of the panel are now visible because the thin layers of oil-paint have become more transparent with age. Some of the underdrawing is visible with the naked eye as bluish grey lines. These are drawn in a sketchy free style and the rhythmic swelling of the line according to the movement of the hand suggests the use of a brush. The underdrawing looks bluish-grey because it is covered by a very thinly applied *imprimatura*. This light grey layer of lead-white and a little carbon black bound in oil has the function of isolating the priming from the paint and serves as a light-reflecting layer. At the first stage of painting the almost white panel was coloured in following the underdrawing with large monochrome areas of colour: warm grey for the town, light green for the grass, and dark grey for the hollows in the terrain. Entire groups of soldiers were underpainted in various shades of grey. In the bottom left corner the grey underpaint for the blue tents is clearly visible. The red and yellow tents have red and yellow underlayers. The main paint-layer shows a remarkable economy of means: the roofs and towers are indicated by dark outlines and highlights in various tones of pink-grey and blue-grey with some dark grey brush-strokes for windows and crenellations. In the same simple way a few pink highlights were sufficient to indicate the soldiers' faces; their armour was painted with white highlights and dark shadows, using the grey underpaint as a middle tone. Banners, the landsknechts' berets and trousers, as well as the horses' splendid saddlecloths, provided scope for accents of red, blue, and yellow. During the last stage the patterns in the flags and saddlecloths were added, like the Habsburg eagle and the French fleurs-de-lis. The final glazes, mainly red and blue in the tents and the saddlecloths, intensify the colour contrasts and give the painting the necessary splendour.

Comparison with the Royal Armouries painting

The Ashmolean *Battle of Pavia* and the one in the Royal Armouries are painted on oak panels of similar size, and the compositions are at first glance almost identical. However, the Armouries painting stresses the siege and

Detail of the Duke of Bourbon, after cleaning, before retouching [left] and after retouching [right].

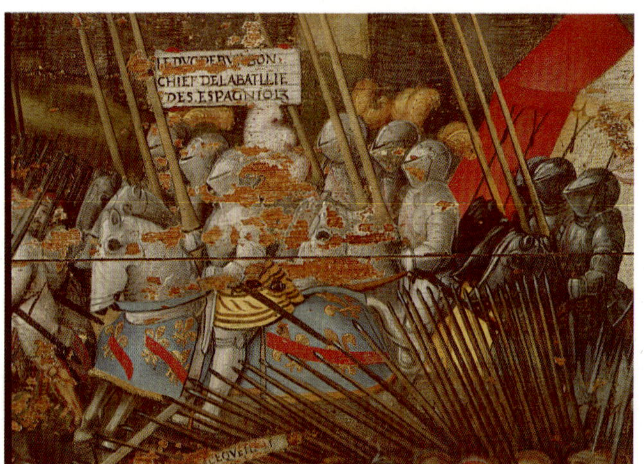

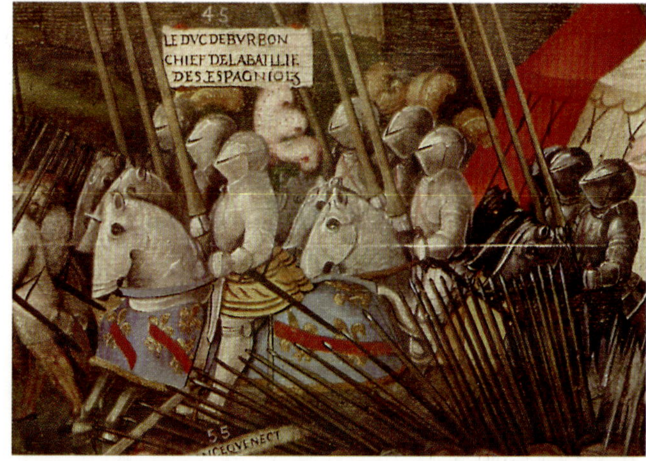

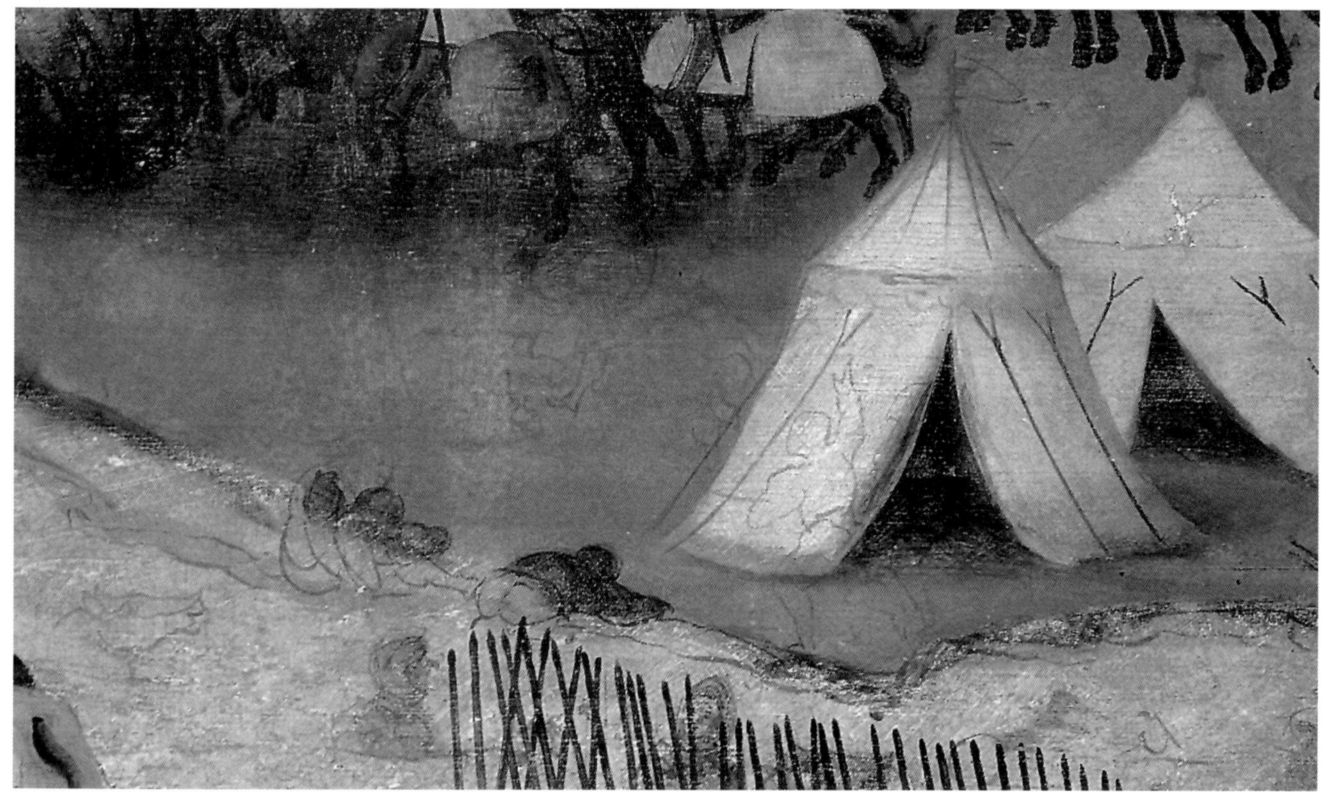

Infra-red reflectograph detail – underdrawing of a man on horseback and two soldiers near the red and yellow tent beyond the river. With infra-red reflectography the absorption of infra-red light by the carbon black of the underdrawing is captured by an infra-red camera.

cannon-fire, whereas the Ashmolean's emphasizes the capture of Francis I. The groups of knights on horseback, landsknechts and halberdiers are the same in both paintings. Tracings made from the Ashmolean painting exactly match the corresponding group of knights on the Armouries picture. There is no doubt that both paintings are based on the same drawings, used for tracing the various elements of the composition onto the primed panels.

Comparison of the infra-red image, showing the underdrawing, of the Ashmolean version with the actual painting revealed remarkable changes between underdrawing and paint-layer. Surprisingly, many of the details in the underdrawing of the Ashmolean painting correspond with the painted details in the Armouries version. The yellow and red paint-layers of the tents on the far side of the river cover the underdrawing of two soldiers. Beneath the green layer of grass next to the tents the outlines of a man on horseback are hidden. The underdrawing for the man sitting sideways on the bank of the river can be seen with the naked eye. In the river above the town the underdrawing of the towers is visible and also the crenellated top of the town-wall. During the painting process the town-wall was lowered to create a more dramatic silhouette. Again, the skyline of the underdrawing corresponds with the painted town in the Armouries picture. There the gate has been seriously damaged and blackened by fire, whereas in the Ashmolean painting only one of the towers is shown with some damage. However, the dark hatching in the underdrawing shows the gate in ruins, as in the Armouries version. The comparison shows that the two paintings are similar in the underdrawing, but that changes were made in the painting of the Ashmolean picture. There is no doubt that both paintings were painted in the same studio. However, whereas the Royal Armouries painting is dramatic and elaborate in every aspect, the Ashmolean one achieves a stronger dramatic effect with economy of detail.

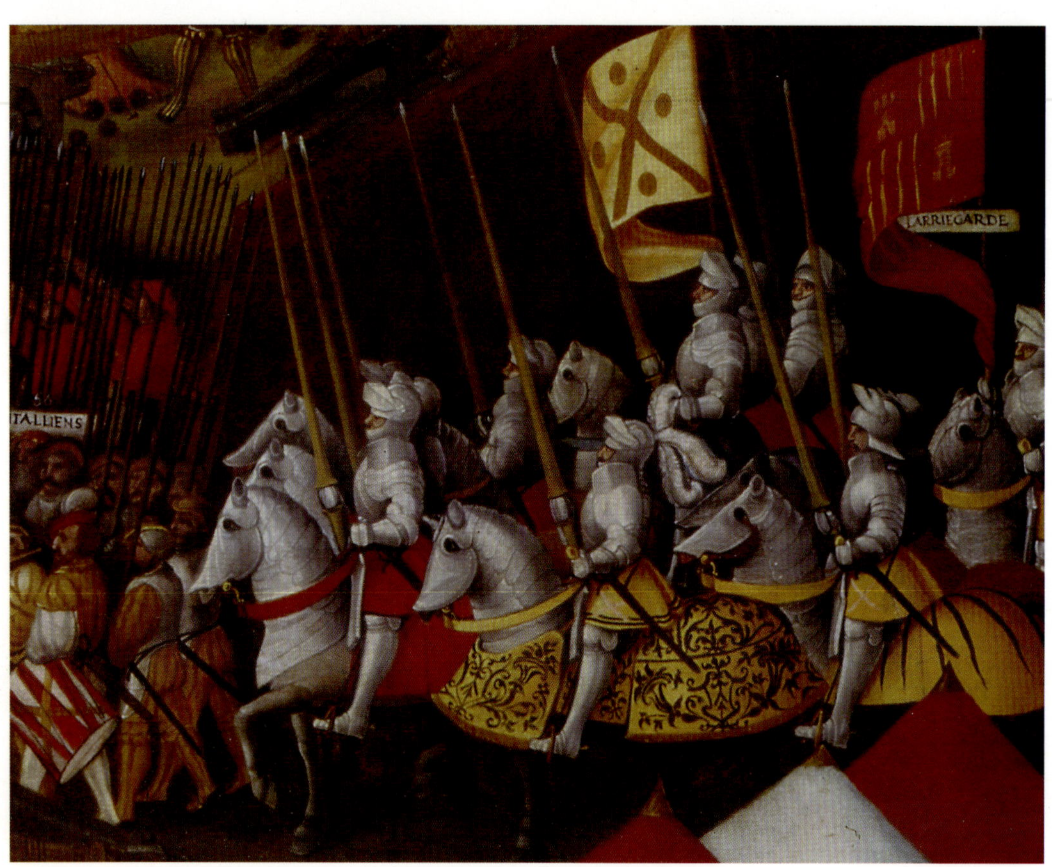

The Imperial rearguard entering the park.